Y0-DDS-937

The Radio Tales

Matthew Kirshman

The Radio Tales
Copyright © Matthew Kirshman

All rights reserved. Red Dashboard LLC
Publishing retains right to reprint.
Permission to reprint story must be
obtained from the author.

ISBN- 13: 978-1502594945

Dime Novel Cover-Art © 2014 Red
Dashboard LLC Publishing

Published by Red Dashboard LLC
Publishing, Princeton, NJ 08540
www.reddashboard.com

to kiersten

The Radio Tales

1

How wrong everything looks this spring.
The sun makes a movie of Abel as he marches
down the street.
He carries a ladder on his back.
His shadow wobbles from the angle
of the evening rays.
The neighborhood was,
but is no longer, charming.
Gardens are charred or covered with trash.
City center is in rubble.
Over all lies a sheet of dust: white atoms
of calcium.
Across Abel's path skulks a human-eyed dog,
its fangs on display.
When the sun sets, a lunar glow rises from the road.
Since the war began, Abel sleeps with an open eye.
And with snipers about, he travels by night.
He became a broker in the black market by chance.
This evening he travels with a packet of meat
against his ribs.
The dog makes a dash toward the scent.
Abel raises an iron pipe and brings it down
on the dog's snout.

The man follows a series of painted arrows
through the streets.
The black market sits at the base of the radio tower.
The lantern-lit crowd greets him like a mute
festivity.
Traders speak through hands and eyes.
Abel concentrates on his work.
He moves through the pack, making the sign for
"tool."
A youth approaches and unfolds a parcel, and at
Abel's feet falls a jumble off hand tools.
He reads the young man's hunger.
Abel shows him the meat.
The kid nods fast.
He accepts a slice, half of which he eats raw
on the spot.
Bartering from hunger, the fool will waste his
goods in hours.
Abel picks a locksmith's kit.
When he looks up, a girl has appeared at the young
man's side.
Her feline eyes take Abel in.
She chews the other bite of meat.
From a deck of tarot cards, she places one in
Abel's palm.
On it is pictured a juggler with two boats behind
him on a swelling sea.
The girl offers to read his fortune for more meat.
Abel's withheld laugh gives him a weird rictus
around the mouth.

Abel signals termination of the trade and vanishes into the knot of dealers.

2

Sam and Marta clung to each other.
They roamed the tent famished for fellowship.
Last night the pair camped in a crater.
Close by came the scraping of little hands.
Boldly, a rat nestled in Sam's sleeping bag.
It raised its head and met the gaze of its hosts.
Sam freed his legs and leapt into Marta's bed.
His jump tipped their lantern, and his toe
inadvertently fanned the cards.
Turning on her belly, Marta drew a row of cards.
Angels swooped in and out of view, influencing
the deck.
Sam looked across the lip of the crater.
His head popped up, level with the street.
People appeared in the rubble, milling for breakfast.
Jet fighters thundered overhead, roaring
toward the radio tower.
He touched Marta, and they rolled up their
belongings.
She signaled for Sam to leave something behind.
They were trekked through trash, uphill.
They passed buildings marked with symbols of war.
Sam's eyes scanned the gravel for metal.
Behind them echoed a megaphone, ordering
campers to disperse.
Sam and Marta sped up.

Voices from the old cinema drew them in.
At the foot of the screen, a man in an old suit
addressed a small audience.
He limped.
Behind him, strokes of day-glow depicted
the radio tower.
He positioned himself before a raised valise.
On it rested a book and handsaw.
The man read with grave cadence.
He opened the suitcase and revealed a lad within.
Your son, your only one, he said, and he closed
the lid of the suitcase.
He angled the saw, and then with a backstroke of
the blade, he cut into the case.
Back and forth, he drew the saw.
Midway, he paused, and then, stroking with force,
he intoned roundly, covering the scream inside.
Sawdust and blood fell in a bowl below.
A larger audience had now gathered.
He stepped back and, pointing to the emblem on the
screen, spoke in unsteady monotone.
Tears streaked the man's face.
Behind him, the screen moved, and a kid's voice
made the man freeze.
He turned and dropped to one knee.
On stage stood the boy—his torn shirt showing a
stomach clotted with sawdust.

3

Graffiti points your way to the underworld.
You go beneath a bed, behind a mirror, or through
an airshaft.
The passage is streaked with color.
You come to a honeycomb of subterranean species.
You move through their burrows on your hands
and knees.
Some nip at you defensively.
The shaft narrows, dead-ending in black.
Then, a turn to the left, and you see a hatch,
a miniature door.
You peer through its keyhole.
Up close is a bird with a golden head.
The bird alights upon a platform, a master of
ceremony, in whose squawk you make out a species
of English.
The bird unveils a woman in a bulb of fire.
She suffers no harm but becomes lovelier
by degree.
She moves in a smoldering gown.
The bird enfolds her smoky body in his wing.
The keyhole frames this magic scene.
You crack the door and see your way inside
a TV studio.
Wires reel the bird to the ceiling.
The manikin lady is wheeled on a dolly.

As she passes through the lights, layers of skin tone are revealed.

A hand on your shoulder hurries you to center stage, before a squad of cameras.

Stagehands set the scene of an operating room.

Magicians, take your places, please.

Four hands lift your body and place it on a gurney.

From above, a camera frames your body.

Next to the operating table plays a radio.

You grin for everyone and give a tiny wave.

Your face is darkened by a gas mask, which emits only air, a placebo.

You feel a wire entering your ear.

The knowledge of the camera's gaze keeps you willingly still.

With a deafening snap, the noise of the world stops.

Someone undoes your shirt.

Blood runs across your chest as surgeons saw into your sternum.

A clamp is applied, and cool air enters your torso.

You feel an outside beat, a cadence entering you.

Cut free, your heart leaps.

An assistant scoops out your heart and places it in a vat by the radio.

A trill enters your ribcage.

Tears rise from your eyes.

The surgeons pull your ribs in place and begin stitching your skin.

The gas is removed, and a tap on the shoulder tells you to stand.

You bow, hearing nothing, while bulbs flash applause.
You glance to the left and see your heart pumping to the radio.

4

A magician made me.
He had a smell of medicine.
One morning, I felt him leave the bed.
I watched him through a veiled-gaze, so he would
not see the light of my look.
He made water in the corner.
I smelled his kidneys in the pot.
Beakers of creatures covered the table.
In a flask, a frog floated, half-asleep in cloudy
liquid.
The frog had a boy's face.
The frog began gazing through the glass.
His look came alive, and his eyes spoke to mine.
Among the beakers, the magician set a book.
His speech rose and fell as it moved through a spell.
He was mixing a potion of powder and spirits.
Smoky figures rose from the mix, and fog formed
above the table.
From the cloud, a gravelly voice materialized.
It went in and out of audibility.
I yawned, stretched, and left the bed.
The odors bothered my stomach, so I made my way
into the hall.
I followed a line of yellow paint: first, to the right
along the hall, and then left down a stairwell.
The stairs came to a T.

I turned left and stopped.

Here was the passage through which I had just come.

Here was our door.

Inside, the magician was chanting, which had an influence on my body.

When I entered, I was induced to drink the potion.

As I drank, a gown covered me.

Images moved up and down the silk.

Scenes shimmered in the fabric: a woman pouring water, a man twirling a stick, a girl guiding a horse.

They came alive for a spell.

The gown glowed as I climbed to the upper world.

I passed the cells of little monsters that snatched at the shining threads.

When I arrived above, my dress was in shreds.

Yet the threads continued to shine.

I heard voices.

Fearing people, I ran down the street, with the dress emitting light about me.

5

Arthur only appeared to work at his station.
He was a prisoner of war.
During shifts, he vanished beneath the factory floor.
A manikin labored in his place.
He inched along airshafts and peered through vents.
He passed the guards' quarters and an electrical
closet.
Through the constricted shaft, his vision was
restricted.
He discovered what looked like a storeroom, whose
shelves were stocked with canned goods.
Below was a table on which lay a ledger.
By the ledger, in an ashtray, a crushed cigarette
smoldered.
Someone had been there a minute ago.
A coat with corporal's stripes was draped over
the back of a chair.
Arthur wished to see the face of this vanished clerk.
An hour went by.
He inched back up the duct.
He returned to his machine as the horn sounded.
He deposited the manikin in a custodial closet and
lined up for roll call.
That night, he dreamt he was inside the storeroom.
He appeared to the clerk as a superior officer.
The clerk was smaller, and Arthur subdued him.

The next morning, the guards called for double quota.

The manikin could not manage the machine at high cycles.

Arthur was forced to work all day.

As the mold parted, he reached in, and a hot cylinder plopped into his hand.

A guard inspected the box of cylinders at Arthur's elbow.

His arms turned leaden from repetition.

Day darkened.

His brain departed his body.

From above, his eye took in the routine of the guards.

In pairs, they rotated through the factory.

Arthur's brain slid under a guard's cap and commanded his body for a minute.

He studied his partner's stride.

He eyed himself working spiritlessly at his station.

What if there was an accident, such as getting his hand caught between the platen?

He returned to his body, with insight into a new plan.

He could make himself look like a manikin.

Then, the guards would move him to the landfill.

6

Abel heads downhill.
A hundred feet ahead sits the shantytown.
Beyond looms the factory, its smokestack making a
dark mark against a grainy sky.
Pre-dawn is black and white.
Shortly, the sun will rise.
Through the air comes the boom of jet fighters.
Two angels orbiting the ladder land on it and
grapple.
Abel traverses a landfill.
A dog barks, and a light flashes in his eye.
A lantern is lifted by Abel's uncle.
The two men meet at a gate.
The uncle guides Abel through the narrow lanes
of the shantytown.
They enter a shack.
A family shares a mattress.
A man cradles a rifle in his sleep.
Abel's aunt lies on a cot with one arm flung to the
floor.
Abel drops his sack to the ground.
His aunt lifts herself up and gives Abel a hug.
His uncle props the cot against the wall.
A hatch is revealed, a door in the floor.
The men descend into a workshop.
In its center sits a rocket, aimed downward.

Abel squeezes into the ship.

The rocket rumbles in the dirt and leaves behind a cloud of dust.

Ghosts floating by mesmerize the pilot.

He is tumbling by old buildings, inhabited by shriveled, elfin men.

He is drifting through a field of fossilized junk.

The ship splashes into an underground lake.

Abel opens the hatch and finds himself in a cavern.

Above him are the bottoms of buildings.

As the ship sinks, Abel paddles across the water.

He follows a footpath along the edge of the lake until he comes to a wall of artifacts.

His way is blocked by paint cans, engine blocks, car doors, washing machines, toilet seats, et cetera.

From a pouch, Abel extracts a locksmith's kit.

He opens a door and slides in.

A radio is playing.

A DJ's velvety voice segues to a song from before the war.

The Badge

Alex Fern woke one morning to the sounds of a bird stirring above his window. At first, it was a shadow of a noise, a part of his dream. Alex was sweeping a floor, sweeping the same spot over and over. He grew annoyed and impatient in his dream. Then his dream gave way to the blue light of morning filtering through his window. The bird was fussing in the rain-gutter, as if she could not make up her mind about something. He wondered if it was building a nest. It was July already. Alex had seen the blue shells of robin's eggs during his walks to the bus stop. Nesting in a rain-gutter was suicide. One day a flood would wash the eggs down the spout. Alex wanted to get out of bed and throw something at the bird. It might think, here's another human trying to kill it, not knowing Alex would be saving it from a worse fate.

His limbs stirring, Alex shifted in bed. There was something wedged between his legs—the cat. Alex's limbs were splayed like scissors. How he slept all night like that, he couldn't imagine. The cat looked like a rabbit, with its all-white fur and pointed ears, and the sun shining through the pink skin, so you could see the veins. The cat's ear twitched, as if it felt Alex's eye. The cat was like

27

Alex's own infant, curled against him like that. If I were a girl, Alex thought, that is where a baby would come out. He wondered what it would be like waking up as a girl. That could happen. Your dick just falls off. In gym, you'd have to shower with your underwear on. But then your voice would get higher and you'd grow a chest and have to start sitting with the girls. He wouldn't need a girlfriend then. He could feel his own chest and kiss his shoulder. If you wanted to touch a girl's hair, you could pretend you were naturally interested in how it was styled and ask her about shampoo. She could tell him deep secrets and that would be like going all the way, sort of. What if he could split in two, and his girl-self slept next to him? He'd already know she liked him and they could have sex. Her body would be his. She'd let him do anything, her eyes saying, it's all right. She would know what he was feeling, and that would be the end of loneliness.

With the radio on, Alex started running in place. When his body warmed up, he lay on the carpet, tucked his feet under the bed and did a hundred sit-ups. After that, he did twenty-five push-ups. He could see the muscles in his torso coming out. His stomach reminded Alex of a photo of his dad as a teenager posing with Alex's grandmother. His dad was wearing shorts and no shirt and had an arm around her. His dad's hair was curly, and he wore a wide smile, even though he was half-naked next to his own mother. They were supposed to have been close. Alex couldn't picture himself with Ma like that, his arm around her and his stomach exposed. Even when he came out of the shower, and walked through the kitchen, he wrapped a towel over his belly button and shawled his shoulders and nipples with another towel. He didn't want Ma to see the waxy hairs climbing his body. Then she'd know he wasn't a boy. She gave birth through a scar in her stomach, and for a long time it was just the two of them. He took care of her by making her laugh with funny voices and characters he made up. That was innocence. But now Alex wanted to have sex with girls and couldn't go around kissing Ma and talking like a little bird.

Alex splashed his face with water. He felt the world warming up and the air getting humid. Some of it was mist left from Ma's shower. On the rim of the sink was a chipped mug with three toothbrushes. They were a family—red, yellow, and blue. Alex was blue. In the medicine cabinet were: Colgate, Scope, Rite Guard, Stan's razor, Barbasol, witch hazel, tweezers, nail polish remover, a hair brush, Q-tips, a nail file, and Ma's pills. Alex studied himself brushing his teeth. He spat a mouthful of froth into the drain and rinsed. He leaned close to the mirror and inspected his mouse like moustache. He remembered sitting next to a kid in science and thinking his new moustache made him look like a Guido. Now it was Alex's turn to show his pubescence to the world. He stepped away from the

29

mirror, raised his fists like a boxer, and began sparring with his reflection. He moved his shoulders side-to-side, bobbing and weaving, and dodging phantom blows. Alex jabbed with his left, snapping it back to keep his guard up. Dancing in place, Alex felt like lightning. Then came his weapon—he faked an uppercut with his left and delivered a roundhouse right. His opponent crumpled. Alex pumped his arms up and down. He was the bantamweight champion of the world! He went to the Olympics and returned to school with a gold medal. It didn't matter he was skinny. He had a killer instinct, and people respected that.

From outside the bathroom, Alex heard a thump. He jumped. He stood alert and listened. All the sound left his body, and his ears stretched to catch a whisper or footfall. Silence came from the other side of the door. He sent mental radar through the five rooms of the house. It was dead out there. Through the window, he heard a dog barking. Down the hill, a woman yelled, and from somewhere else a kid shouted back. He heard the racket of a hammer, a thwack and then its echo. He could hear the whole neighborhood and wondered why noise was so full in summertime, but in winter sound sounded muffled. When he had stood on the cliff, he could hear people on the lake. One time, he saw John and Peter in the boat. The motor had stalled, John was standing and pulling the cord over and over, and each time he pulled, he swore Christ!

Piss! until he finally stopped and stood in the rocking boat with his head down. Peter had started talking, and Alex had known it was Peter by bits of his voice. You could tell barking dogs from one another by their tone, but you could tell people by their cadence, even from a murmur.

Alex peered through the bathroom door: no one there, but the cat looking up at him. If there was a prowler in the house, the cat would be hiding under the table, not gazing up with that love-me-forever look. Then Alex saw the source of the thump. The cat had knocked a potted plant to the floor. The terracotta pot lay in two pieces, it soil bleeding onto the carpet, and the coleus sprawled out like a drowning swimmer. The cat rubbed against Alex's legs, so that when he started walking, he stumbled and cried out, "C'mon, Gilligan, get out of here," and gave the cat a poke with his toe. The cat purred like a motor. There was a note on the refrigerator. Alex loved letters and secret messages. By the writing, he knew the note was from Ma. Some of her letters were loopy, while others were sticks. Alex hoped she wrote something personal, or some strange and liberating fact—the secret of his birth, or the announcement of an important trip that only he would be going on. Here is a thousand dollars, Alex, for you to go to Europe. We'll miss you but have a good time. Love, Ma. Instead the note said,

Al, do DISHES empty TRASH and Mow LAWN.

The well-room where they kept the lawnmower was full of spider webs. The space was damp and crumbly. The well-room belonged to another century. It was historic, there were no cement walls, and you could see the dirt and rocks upon which the house was built. It was called the well-room because that was where water from a well was pumped into the house. It was weird to think there was water underground that belonged to them. How much water was down there? Where did it come from so there was always more? Once, something went wrong with the pump, and Stan had to dig a trench. He had gotten dirty and frustrated because he hadn't known where the pump was buried. By the time he'd found it, Stan had looked grim, and he'd staggered from the trench holding the pump like a creature. Yard tools were thrown in the well-room too, in no real order. No one bothered. Parts of the yard were overgrown. Where the previous owners had bred here and there a nice bed of flowers, nature now took over. Alex lugged the lawnmower across a rocky patch to the driveway. Twice he yanked the cord grunting, his shoulder jerking out of joint with the cord's retraction. On the third pull, the motor started with a roar.

* * *

Alex wheeled his ten-speed from the shed. He'd left it in tenth gear, so when he headed downhill, he wouldn't have to shift, but could just start pedaling hard. He'd fly past Esperanza's house, and then as he hit the bend, he'd glide into the trees along a straight stretch of road. It was a good bike, though not as nice as Peter's. Whenever they raced, Peter creamed him. His was a lightweight twelve-speed with toe clips and Shimano derailleurs. Last summer, Peter had ridden through the Catskills. For two weeks he'd just ridden and camped with strangers. He'd gotten ready for the trip by climbing the hills in their neighborhood. One Saturday, Alex had been inside, with his Bar Mitzvah tutor. Sitting at the dining room table, reading from a photocopied bit of the Torah, he looked up every ten minutes to see if there was Pete whizzing by the house. Now, Alex pushed off with one foot, and mounting his bike while it was rolling, threw a leg over it. The wind rushed across his ears. He crouched low, tucked his head above the handlebars. As he rounded the bend, his eyes were alive to signs of sand. He flew into shadows, through shafts of sunlight. He breezed by the boulders leading up to the cliff. He sped by the backyard where that old collie always lay; she didn't have time to start barking. Slowing, Alex stuck his foot against the tar and pivoted into the second bend. He headed downhill, the box-like houses blurring in the corner of his eye. He skidded to a stop at the firehouse and collected his breath. Before him, lay Secret Lake, wisps of mist rising from its silver surface.

John Shortell was in the garage fixing his old outboard motor, the green finish peeling away, its Mercury logo barely visible. The motor, clamped to a workbench, had its hood removed. It looked like an exposed skull. Alex imagined making a robot with all these spare bike and engine parts. He would need cables and little gears. He would want the robot to make delicate maneuvers, like scratching its nose or tying its shoes. John blew through a plastic tube. He'd taken apart the carburetor for the hundredth time. Its pieces were spread out on newspaper. He picked up a valve and held it to the light. The valve looked like a pair of wings. He asked Alex, "Did you hear about the guy who loved his motorcycle so much they got married?"

"Really?" asked Alex, credulously. "Wow—That's true love."

"Yeah—They exchanged piston rings!"

John repeated the punch line and laughed hilariously, as if there were some hidden dimension in it. Alex considered the joke, frustrated he didn't know what piston rings were and figured you'd have to be as turned on by machines as John was to really get the joke.
"How would they have sex?" Alex asked.

John gave a snort. He was looking at a tiny spring that was fastened to the valve. He tugged at the spring, and the valve squeaked open. John placed the valve upon a little rod inside a metal cup and hooked the spring through a tiny eyelet. Wearing a serious look, he examined the mechanism and, tapping the valve with a pencil, watched it open and close. Then he barked, "Shot to shit!"

"What's wrong?" Alex asked worriedly.

"The spring—it's shot. Shot to shit. Shit and double shit!"

"That's not a big deal is it, a spring?"

"Yessss," John hissed, then slipped into silence.

John had black crescent moons of grease under his fingernails. He wore a tank top, and tufts of hair bristled from his armpits. But the rest of his body was smooth. Wispy sideburns grew along his jaw. In his knee-length cut-offs, he looked a gangly clown. The way John lunged about his garage Alex thought any moment an accident might happen. John might elbow something in the clutter, sending everything toppling like a domino. When they rode their ten-speeds, Alex pedaled behind him and would watch John's knees as they sliced the air. Once John took off, he soared, his long hair flying. No one could catch him, even though his bike was cobbled from junk. John bent over an old lawnmower, going at it with a socket wrench. He worked without a word. Usually he talked non-stop, seeming to need company always. You'd start out thinking, because of his ardent tone, he was telling you something major. But if you followed what he was saying, after a while you'd figure out there was really no point to it. It was stuff going in all directions.

John tore apart a lawnmower in furious silence. Alex walked circles around the garage, picking things up and putting them down, curious about the gadgetry. He crisscrossed his palm with a greasy sprocket. He glanced over at John, worried by his dark mood.

"You know that Who song 'See Me, Feel Me'?" Alex asked.

"Hmmm."

"Yeah," Alex continued, "it's in Pete's songbook. It's really cool, because it's like two different songs in one. I was playing it a little bit, but the chords are hard. They're not just like E and A. It's complex."

"Chaz saw them," John said without looking up.
 "They were drunk."

"All except for the bass player, I bet. He just stands there like a scarecrow."

"Acid. All those guys dropped acid."

"Oh, yeah," said Alex, as if he'd known this fact all his life. "If Chaz was drunk, how'd he know they were too?"

"Maybe," replied John, holding in the air a tiny spring that he'd just removed from the lawnmower's carburetor, "maybe they were *more* drunk."

After his brothers left home, John inherited a garage full of treasure: a canoe, camping gear, fishing rods, a drum set, a bass amp, a movie camera, records, a go-cart, a chemistry set, Mad magazines, and board games. He closed his eyes and strummed his fingers across an Ouija board to see if it gave off any mystic signals. To Alex, it was enticing—the garage stuff could keep you busy for a hundred years. Alex fiddled with the knob of a gas lantern. Inside the globe, hung a delicate piece of cloth. When lit, the flame hovered amid the gauze without burning it. The lantern sat atop a compact stove, one burner attached to a cylinder of gas. Alex imagined running away, living on the cliff in a tent and reading comic books and *Mad* magazine by lantern-light. Alex approached the workbench and, leaning on his elbows, watched John reassemble the motor. John plucked nuts, screws and washers from their separate piles.

"I bet you could do that blindfolded," said Alex.

"I could do it blindfolded with no hands walking on a tightrope," said John.

"Not bad."

"Not good either."

"Why?"

"Because now the lawnmower's broken."

* * *

Together, Alex and John carried the motor down to the lake. The boat lay in the grass to the left of the beach. Two docks reached into the water, with a yellow rope of blue and white buoys drawn between them. A boy and a girl were in the swimming area.

"Look, grandma, look! Watch me do a handstand!"

Grandma, grandma, grandma, grandma! I can do an underwater somersault!"

"Count how long I can hold my breath!"

The grandmother stood at the water's edge, nodding.

Not far a lifeguard, watching, the action from a low chair on the sand, or seemed to be, through mirrored sunglasses. To the right of the beach sat a picnic table. Nearby, in the dirt, was a charred circle, in which remained a blackened, half-consumed log. Between the water and the table stood a tree, upon whose bark hung a sign saying *No Fires*.

Fat clouds hung over the hill on the far side of the lake. But the air was still, and if the clouds held rain, they did not appear to be moving. The two kids flew off the dock and cried in unison—

"Cannonball!"

Alex and John planted the motor beside the boat and approached the lifeguard.

"Some people have no consideration for sleep," said John.

"Yeah," Vera laughed. "Could you set them straight?"

Alex pointed to the raft. He asked, "How fast could you swim out there if he started drowning?"

"Probably not very," said the lifeguard, Vera.

"I wouldn't even leave my seat," said John.

"Would you lose your job if he died?" asked Alex.

She laughed, "I'd have to look like I was trying."

"Did you hear about the time Vera swam three-quarters to the raft, got tired and swam back?" John trumpeted: "Then she got nearly back to the beach, realized she'd been closer to the raft and swam back!"

"I'm surprised you ever made it to shore," said Alex.

"John saved me," she said.

They slid the boat alongside the dock. Alex, kneeling on the dock, steadied the boat, while John, waded in the water, then mounted the motor. Alex felt the bow push up against his hands. The shore on the far side of the dock was mucky. Sunlight spreading through the water made the muck shimmer; the bubbles, like tiny pearls glistened among its fibers. Alex watched a school of minnows glide in and out of the shadow of the dock. Snapping turtles lived in the lake and laid eggs in the algae. When he swam, even if his own toe brushed his leg, a primal part of him believed it was a snapping turtle. John stepped into the boat and with one momentous pull started the motor. It coughed clouds of blue stinging smoke. Alex looked at John with raised eyebrows.

"Have faith!" he shouted over the motor. "Get in!"

The boat chugged forward, leaving dock and beach behind. The kids in the swimming area staring as the two sailors grew smaller. Vera, through her silver shades gazed goodbye. The boat bouncing along the surface baptized the boys with spray. A dragonfly zigzagged before the oncoming bow. The lake smelled alive. They were headed diagonally from the beach toward the center of the lake. Alex's eyes skimmed the little homes along the edge. There was Pete's backyard, where they played football. Pete's Sunfish lay on its side, the yellow sail spread carelessly in the dirt. There was the rope-swing. Next time he'd fly off the swing and splay into the water like he was born for it. Toward the skinny end of the lake, where cattails and lily pads grew, stood Finnegan's: the home of Pete's enemy. They erupted in fists every year going back to a Jewish slur Finnegan had made. In Finnegan's backyard, along the water's edge, a dog stood barking, its jaws going up and down, its yelp drowned out by the motor.

Alex turned to look at John, who with one hand steered and with another hand brushed the hair from his eyes. John's shirt was spotted with spray. He called to Alex, his voice muffled by the motor.

"…ereht…ait…it…et!"

Alex shrugged and turned up his palms. He put on a helpless expression and mouthed the words, "I can't understand you."

John killed the motor.

"I said, a *perfect place for a cigarette*!"

Little waves kissed the side of the boat, rocking it. If the lake had been a man, they'd paused at his stomach. From here you could see the cliff: a shelf of rock topped by trees. Crouching in the rocking boat, John rooted through his pockets and extracted a plastic sandwich bag wrapped into a tight cylinder. On his knee, he unfolded the bag, gazing at its contents critically. There were three stubbed cigarettes, a book of matches, rolling papers and a finger's worth of pot. Alex's eyes widened at the sight of the herb. Stan smoked all the time. It gave Alex butterflies, having friends who got high in the woods and at the beach at night. John withdrew two of the cigarette stubs, tucked them in his mouth, and replaced the stash in his pocket. Then, bending low, so that his head was sheltered from the wind, John struck a match and lifted the cupped flame to his mouth. Up he jerked like a jack-in-the-box. The cigarettes jutted from the corners of his mouth like two smoking tusks.

Alex laughed. "Did you know smoking's bad for you?"

The wind carried off Alex's voice. He could hardly hear himself. He could not bring himself to shout. It would wreck the serenity of this scene.

"It could be the manifold," said John, his voice pitched above the wind.

"The manifold?" Alex said quietly. He didn't understand. He thought of all the things surrounding them—the clouds, the houses on one side of the lake, the rushes on the other, and the kids in the swimming area. They were manifold.

"An air leak probably," said John. "Don't you think it's still running rich?"

"Could be," said Alex.

"I can't get the gaskets, but we could seal around it temporarily and take it for another test ride. Just to see."

"Yeah."

What was John talking about? Who was he talking to? John's obsession with the engine invaded Alex's head, ruining the nice feeling he'd had about the lake. It made Alex angry. Bikes and cars were all John cared about, gears going round and round, pistons going up and down, in monotonous, robotic repetition. He was chewing Alex's ear. Alex's spirits sank. He felt distant on his side of the boat.

Timeline

June 1965—A young man in white shirt and trousers admitted himself to Connecticut Valley Hospital. A week earlier, JK thought about killing himself. Now, he felt in a suspended state, like a dead person, and he said that unless the nerves and muscles in his legs were replaced, there would be no future for him. JK was not hearing voices. But people were using a symbolic language. *They were shaking their heads*, he said. *And one of them was moving his right arm, which meant that my right leg should be done in the same way as my left leg. After a while, he was walking like a pretzel.* Asked about his concentration, JK said, *Everything is happening at the same time.*

A month before his marriage, JK began a system of breathing. He would stand straight and inflate his stomach, and while breathing he felt his kidneys moving up and down his back. It was warm and pleasant. It influenced women in a positive way. But he noticed it had a bad effect on men. At work, a man approached him, and he felt his intestines drawing forward. He could not keep them in. He saw hate in the faces of the other men. Along his legs he felt balls of fire, which he said were the cause of his problem.

47

December 1988—A University of Connecticut student sat in his dorm room with his hands on a typewriter. Nearby was a bottle of wine. MK was arguing against the rationale of private language: that one's talk is like walking through a gallery of paintings whose images are meaningful only to a single gazer. It was Friday night, and the dorm was noisy. Down the hall, kids were partying—grain alcohol and punch. MK saw girls spinning out of control. The young man tried to be logical. He built one phrase upon another. The wine felt warm as it entered his system. He waded into his philosophy paper. He was pregnant with a kind of structure. He guided his reader through a house of words. In this room, he said what he meant by *recognize* and *identify*. In the next room, he said what he meant by *having a sensation*. He wanted to show that behind the act of naming—*e.g., rifle, tiger, red,* and *pain*—was an institution of gestures and signs. *All talk has a public interpretation.* What MK said was sensible, but the phrases came from an unknown plane. Someone inside told his hands what to write.

March 1966—JK returned to the world outside the hospital. Throughout his care, he was argumentative and testing, looking for improvement in terms of change in his somatic system. He seemed unable to hear concerns about his unreadiness for fatherhood. In outpatient therapy, JK and his wife questioned their marriage. Each felt alone. They never hau sex. Both felt unless he was able to improve from his condition of not being able to give and receive love, it would be better for her and the baby to be separated from him. He earned a living as a dishwasher, then worked in a factory. He stayed home and slept. Finally, he returned to the bakery, which—with the pressure of working alongside Dad—intensified his anger. They argued in the kitchen, two men dusty with flour. His mother came between them. JK took an interest in cake decoration. He enjoyed working in his own space, away from his father's voice.

September 1989—MK entered journalism by chance. He earned $25 an article for The Chronicle.

STORRS—*A hooded woman perches on stilts. She holds the head of a horse in the air. A trailing white sheet is carried by children, who pretend they are the horse's legs. She describes herself as "a walking stage, a visible puppeteer, doing puppetry the way it was traditionally done, when the lips were not supposed to be unseen." She employs a kind of symbolism, making emotions and personality graphic with as few effects as possible. By exaggerating some movements and simplifying others, she pares the action of a puppet down to the pure essentials.*

Once, he was given a key to The Herald to type at night his own report. He saw the words as emblems, whose ancestry bridged broadcast news to archaic thought. The true life of the words hovered above their context. As correspondent for The Journal, MK earned $30 per story. The editor seldom changed a word, which pleased the young writer, because inside the language were hints of Thought Structure. In a feature on North East Helicopter, MK evoked Daedalus's winged flight across the sea and Elijah's chariot ride into heaven. While MK had eternity in mind, the flight instructor supplied the gravity of the story.

Although the picture of spiraling to earth from a great height might seem like the most unnerving possibility in being a flight instructor, "most of the problems occur two or three feet above the ground—the ground being the main obstruction," he said. In turbulent wind, especially near the ground where the wind can shift unpredictably, "the machine has a pendular effect. Learning how to hover a helicopter, especially a light one, is like learning to ride a unicycle up a frozen wall with a bald tire," he said.

November 1968—JK stopped taking medication. It made him sick. He quit work and started talking like Jesus Christ. His mother called the police. JK was taken to the emergency room of New Britain

General, which transferred him to CVH. JK was described as a drowsy, unkempt, slouching young man who talked in a grandiose, stilted manner. He said he was hearing Jehovah's voice. I was brought. People break me down and bother me. He rambled on about his rule over everyone. I was here once before. He recalled being crucified. High doses of tranquilizers for agitation. Closed ward. While on the ward, JK was aloof and did not socialize with other patients. He was not a problem in handling. Once, he walked out without telling anybody, but came back on his own.

July 1993—A hit of pot before MK left home. Altered Thought. He imagined himself another person—father's silent partner. Aim to drink where there're chicks, no pick-up plan. *Safety mechanism says when to stop, before dark half makes trouble. One beer: cowl of jokes and drama cloaks me: drawling, snickering privacies. Asylum Street, Hartford: father's last days, diseased, wandering. Grown-up son. Mirror above bar, spy father's lips, chin. Smile, welcome back. Wander through drizzle to next bar. Second crowd suits me, milling strangers. Own world, drowned-out TV. Vision's doubling, slow-motion flames, dancing couples. Silent howl of bodies stills me. Three women, fancy eyes. Desire loops silver belt round trim waist. Dude across, trying small-talk, finds ironic tone tedious. Near broke, want last drink near home,* *case sex falls close to cave.   Wait for bus in rain, by hotel where father ended life.   No bus.   Tears on cheeks.   Anger & alcohol haunting system. Hallucinatory, poisoned cells, blind, going mad?*

January 1971—When JK returned to CVH, there were two non-sutured, mending lacerations on his right forearm. He spoke of reaching his vital self. A few days earlier, JK had shaved his head. He said his hair had been long, and he wanted to know what he really looked like. He decided he looked funny and felt that the act of shaving his head indicated to him that he was getting sicker. He related in a friendly, but reserved way, and he smiled strangely, at his own thoughts. He was afraid of walking down the street and talking aloud to his voices. In the past, his voices told him to harm himself, but now they kept him company, making amusing remarks. *When I was reading a book, words were reading for me.* He reported hearing music. Other people were repeating his thoughts. Once in the street, he saw a gazelle lift its head and gaze at him. He could smell perfume and wine.

September 1994—MK returned home. With his eyes closed, he listened to jays shrieking in backyard hemlock. He sat cross-legged in semi-shadows, note-taking from I Ching, his notepad shielding him from anxiety. He honed himself to non-being. *I would like to extract myself bit-by-bit until I am left with the essential facts of the world. Subsume my personality to outer objects: railing, crooked branch, window.* The phone rang and MK answered it like one dream-plucked. He was distant to the caller.

February 1973—JK was interviewed at the New Haven Halfway House and accepted on a one-week trial. At the end of the week, the house members would vote on accepting or rejecting him. JK worried they would not like him. He forgot to care for his appearance—no socks, untied shoes, heavy body odor. His appearance was so run down, he went to the Salvation Army and received clothing. This helped build his self-esteem. The counselor at the house stated that JK would be staying on. He was happy and eager to make it. He would do volunteer work at a bakery in the city.

Author's Biography

Matthew Kirshman lives in Seattle, Washington with his wife and two daughters. He is an English teacher, but before that had a varied career–telephone repairman, bartender, and cook, to name a few. Writing since the early 1980s, his publication credits include: *Altpoetics, Annapurna Magazine, Apeiron Review, Ascent Aspirations, The Bacon Review, BlazeVOX, Café Irreal, Commonline Journal, Cordite, Dirigible, Futures Trading, Helix, Indefinite Space, Key Satch(el), Mad Hatters' Review, Phoebe, posthumous papers (NothingNew Press), Vangarde Magazine, The Wayfarer, Wilderness House Literary Review, Xenarts, and Z-Composition.*

THE DIME NOVEL IS MAKING A COMEBACK!

Originating in the late 19th-century and seeing its heyday in the 1940s and 1950s, particularly in genres such as the Western, the format became an important influence on the comic book, the radio drama, and the film and television treatment. Today's "flash novel" is really a new take on an old idea: stories just shy of novelette length, with numbered chapters rather than asterisks, and which, like the movies, compress a narrative otherwise "novelistic" in scope into a short form suitable for a single reading or download.

Red Dashboard LLC is a small indie publishing house seeking intriguing books of poetry and literature: poetry (chapbook and full-length), flash and short story collections, non-fiction, black-and-white artwork.

THE DESERT DIME NOVEL TRILOGY

by M.V. Montgomery

BOOK 1

Mark Twain in Outer Space is a comic space western featuring a not-so-innocent abroad. It also offers a serious reflection upon the universality of storytelling, and the dangers of getting carried away with the sound of one's own words.

BOOK 2

The Double Dare Devil features Skip Eubanks, an old cowboy-turned-stuntman who is paralyzed after a fall from a helicopter. His wife Bonnie now runs the business, but something very sinister is happening to the stuntmen she supplies to the studios.

BOOK 3

Trouble in Paradise Valley tells the story of a big budget Hollywood production that somehow survives star egos, several rewrites, and its own faulty premise. But how long can it last when it intrudes onto a site once sacred to Hohokam skywatchers

OTHER DIME NOVEL SERIES

www.reddashboard.com

16422553R00039

Made in the USA
San Bernardino, CA
01 November 2014